GEORGE AND MARTHA ENCORE

BY JAMES MARSHALL

A TRUMPET CLUB SPECIAL EDITION

For Adolph, Adrienne,
Ronald, and Philip

Published by The Trumpet Club
a division of Bantam Doubleday Dell Publishing Group, Inc.
666 Fifth Avenue, New York, New York 10103

ISBN: 0-440-84158-5

Reprinted by arrangement with Houghton Mifflin Company
Printed in the United States of America
January 1990

10 9 8 7 6 5 4 3 2 1
UPC

MORE STORIES ABOUT TWO GREAT CHUMS

~

STORY NUMBER ONE

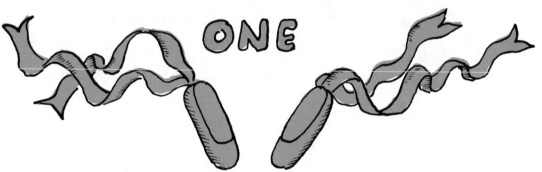

THE DANCE RECITAL

George and Martha were having a disagreement.

"I think dancing is dumb," said George.

"Dancing is not dumb!" exclaimed Martha.

"Dancing is fun! And if you don't come to my dance recital, I'll be very angry!"

So, of course, George went to Martha's recital.

"I'm going to hate this," he said to himself.

But what a surprise for George!

Martha's Dance of the Happy Butterfly

was so impressive.

"Dancing looks like fun," said George.

The next day George went to dancing class.

"You see," said Martha, "dancing is fun!"

Very soon George was in his own dance recital.
Martha said that his Mexican Hat Dance was
the best she had ever seen.

THE SECOND STORY

THE FRENCH LESSON

George went to Martha's house for his French lesson.

"Bonjour, Martha," said George.

"Bonjour, George," said Martha.

George sat next to Martha on the sofa.

"How do you say 'Give me a kiss' in French?" asked George.

"You say 'Voulez-vous m'embrasser?*' " answered Martha.

And that is just what George did.

"Tee-hee," said Martha.

"I knew you were going to do that."

STORY NUMBER THREE

THREE

THE DISGUISE

George decided to dress up as an Indian.

"This disguise will really fool Martha," he chuckled.

"She'll never recognize me."

But Martha wasn't fooled a bit.

"Hi, George," she said.

"Why are you wearing that Indian costume?"

George was so disappointed.

He walked away hanging his head.

Martha felt simply awful.

She hadn't meant to hurt George's feelings.

"George," said Martha. "I would never have recognized

you if it hadn't been for your bright smiling eyes.

It's so hard to disguise smiling eyes."

And, of course, George felt much, much better.

STORY NUMBER FOUR

THE BEACH

One day George and Martha went to the beach.

"I love the beach!" exclaimed Martha.

"So do I," said George.

"However, we must be sure to put on our suntan lotion."

But Martha refused to put on her suntan lotion.

"You'll be sorry," George called out.

"Oh, pooh," said his friend.

"You're a fuss-budget, George."

Martha was having such a lovely time.

The next day Martha had a terrible sunburn!

She felt all hot and itchy.

But George never said "I told you so."

Because that's not what friends are for.

THE LAST STORY

STORY

THE GARDEN

Martha was so discouraged.

Her garden was an ugly mess of weeds.

"I just don't seem to have a green thumb," she sobbed.

George hated to see Martha unhappy.

He wanted so much to help.

Suddenly George had a splendid idea.

He went to the florist and bought

all the tulips in the shop.

Tulips were Martha's favorite flowers.

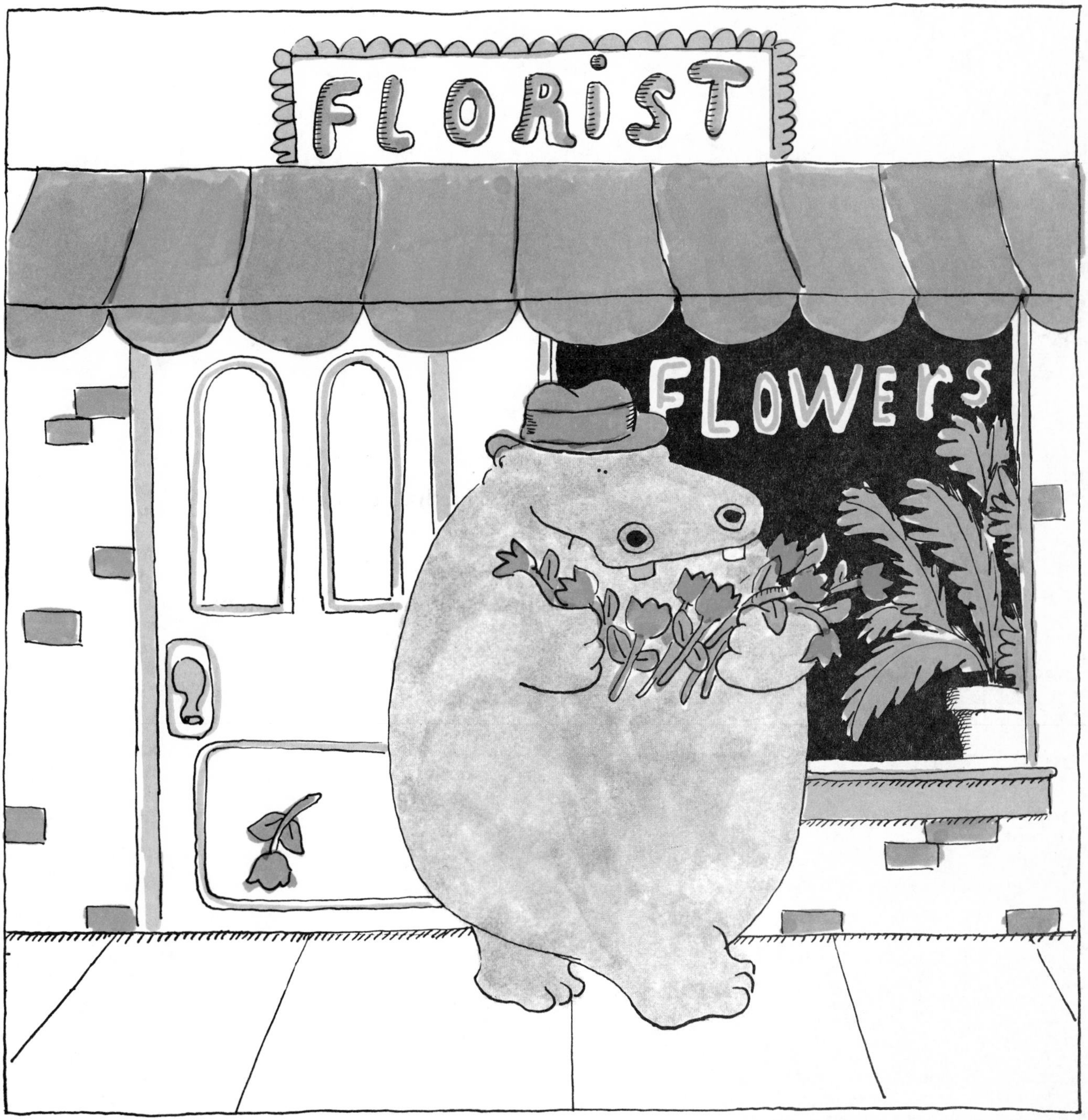
FLORIST
FLOWERS

Very quietly George crept into Martha's garden

and stuck the tulips in the ground.

But just then Martha happened to look out the window.

"Oh, dear," said George.

"You're always catching me."

But Martha was so pleased.

"Dear George," she said.

"I would much rather have a friend like you

than all the gardens in the world."